W9-CAG-470

THE ZACK FILES

Just Add Water... and Scream!

LETTERS TO DAN GREENBURG
ABOUT THE ZACK FILES:

From a mother in New York, NY: "Just wanted to let you know that it was THE ZACK FILES that made my son discover the joy of reading...I tried everything to get him interested...THE ZACK FILES turned my son into a reader overnight. Now he complains when he's out of books!"

From a boy named Toby in New York, NY: "The reason why I like your books is because you explain things that no other writer would even dream of explaining to kids."

From Tara in Floral Park, NY: "When I read your books I felt like I was in the book with you. We love your books!"

From a teacher in West Chester, PA: "I cannot thank you enough for writing such a fantastic series."

From Max in Old Bridge, NJ: "I wasn't such a great reader until I discovered your books."

From Monica in Burbank, IL: "I read almost all of your books and I loved the ones I read. I'm a big fan! *I'm Out of My Body, Please Leave a Message*. That's a funny title. It makes me think of it being the best book in the world."

From three mothers in Toronto: "You have managed to take three boys and unlock the world of reading. In January they could best be characterized as boys who 'read only under duress.' Now these same guys are similar in that they are motivated to READ."

From Stephanie in Hastings, NY: "If someone didn't like your books that would be crazy."

From Dana in Floral Park, NY: "I really LOVE I mean LOVE your books. I read them a million times. I wish I could buy more. They are so good and so funny."

From a teacher in Pelham, NH: "My students are thoroughly enjoying [THE ZACK FILES]. Some are reading a book a night."

From Madeleine in Hastings, NY: "I love your books...I hope you keep making many more Zack Files."

THE ZACK FILES™

Just Add Water... and Scream!

By Dan Greenburg

Illustrated by Jack E. Davis

GROSSET & DUNLAP • NEW YORK

GREAT NECK LIBRARY

For Judith, and for the real Zack,
with love—D.G.

I'd like to thank my editor
Jane O'Connor, who makes the process
of writing and revising so much fun,
and without whom
these books would not exist.

I also want to thank
Emily Sollinger and Megan Bryant
for their terrific ideas.

Text copyright © 2002 by Dan Greenburg. Illustrations copyright © 2002 by Jack E. Davis.
All rights reserved. Published by Grosset & Dunlap, a division of Penguin Putnam Books
for Young Readers, 345 Hudson Street, New York, NY 10014. GROSSET & DUNLAP and
THE ZACK FILES are trademarks of Penguin Putnam Inc. Published simultaneously in
Canada. Printed in the U.S.A.

Library of Congress Cataloging-in-Publication Data

Greenburg, Dan.
    Just add water—and scream! / by Dan Greenburg ; illustrated by Jack E. Davis.
        p. cm. — (The Zack files ; 29)
    Summary: Zack, his father, and Spencer fight to save the world from a rude, bossy,
and hungry package of freeze-dried spores purchased at The Orville and Fanny
Shlectwasser Museum of Air and Space.   [1. Extraterrestrial beings—Fiction.
2. Humorous stories.] I. Davis, Jack E., ill. II. Title.
PZ7.G8278 Jw 2003
[Fic]—dc21
                                                                    2002151424

ISBN 0-448-42887-3   A B C D E F G H I J

Chapter 1

Up until a few days ago, the only space alien I ever met was polite and well-behaved. So I stopped being afraid of space aliens, and I actually looked forward to meeting more of them. Then a visit to the Orville and Fanny Shlectwasser Museum of Air and Space changed everything.

Before we go into that, I'd better tell you who I am and stuff.

My name is Zack. I'm ten-going-on-eleven, and I'm in the fifth grade at the Horace Hyde-White School for Boys.

That's in New York City. My parents are divorced, and I spend about half my time with each of them. It's when I'm staying with my dad that all the weird stuff happens. Like the time I was going to tell you about.

My friend Spencer and I were doing some research for a science project on astronauts. Our science teacher, Mrs. Coleman-Levin, was planning to take our class to Washington, D.C., so we could visit the National Air and Space Museum, part of the Smithsonian Institution. But that wasn't for another month or so. In the meantime, one Saturday, Spencer and I decided to start our research at the museum in New York.

The Orville and Fanny Shlectwasser Museum of Air and Space is on West 99th Street, on the Upper West Side of Manhattan. It's in the basement of an old brownstone, in the apartment of Orville and Fanny Shlectwasser. Mr. Shlectwasser was the former janitor at the National Air and Space Museum in Washington. Almost all the exhibits in the Shlectwasser museum are ones the Smithsonian in Washington didn't want.

For example, they have used Apollo astronaut handkerchiefs with real astronaut boogers. They have discarded Russian cosmonaut underpants from the Soyuz space station.

The Smithsonian Air and Space Museum in Washington has a Mercury space capsule that came back from outer space. The Shlectwasser has mercury from a broken astronaut thermometer.

The Smithsonian has the actual centrifuge machine that whirls astronaut trainees around and around until they vomit. The Shlectwasser has a bucket of actual astronaut trainee vomit.

The Smithsonian has a space suit worn

by Neil Armstrong when he first walked on the moon. The Shlectwasser has a T-shirt worn by Neil Armstrong's nephew after his uncle came back. It says "My uncle walked on the moon, and all I got was this lousy T-shirt."

Spencer and I were kind of disappointed in the Shlectwasser museum, but we didn't want to hurt the feelings of Mr. and Mrs. Shlectwasser.

"So how did you like it?" asked Mrs. Shlectwasser.

She was about four and a half feet tall, and about four and a half feet wide.

"I liked it a lot," I said.

"What did you like in particular?" asked Mr. Shlectwasser.

He was about six foot seven, and about two feet wide. He had an Adam's apple the size of a nectarine.

"The, uh, Apollo handkerchiefs would have to be *my* favorites," I said.

"Oh, those are real honeys," he said. "By the way, those are genuine astronaut boogers. Did you know that?"

"Yes, I did," I said. "That's what the sign said."

He turned to Spencer.

"And you, son?" he said. "What was *your* favorite?"

"I guess mine would have to be the, uh, cosmonaut underpants, sir," said Spencer.

"Aren't they beauties?" said Mr. Shlectwasser. "They're made out of fur, because of the cold winters they have in Russia. And in space, of course."

"Well, we'd better be on our way," I said. "We don't want to miss our subway."

"Don't the subways pretty much run one right after the other?" asked Mrs. Shlectwasser.

"Pretty much," I said.

"Then before you go, you have to time to stop in our lovely gift shop," said Mrs. Shlectwasser.

I looked at Spencer. He shrugged. I really didn't have the heart to say no to her.

"Sure," I said.

The Shlectwasser Air and Space Museum Gift Shop wasn't any better than the museum. Spencer bought a T-shirt that said "My uncle went to the Orville and Fanny Shlectwasser Air and Space Museum, and all I got was this lousy T-shirt." I bought some foil packets of freeze-dried astronaut food—some sausage-and-pepperoni pizza, some strawberry ice cream, some s'mores.

At least I *thought* that was what I bought. What I actually bought almost ended life on Earth as we know it.

Chapter 2

By the time Spencer and I got back to Dad's apartment it was almost four p.m.

"I'm hungry," said Spencer. "You got anything to eat?"

We went into the kitchen. On the kitchen table was my laptop computer. I had left it on, but I always do that. I went to the refrigerator, opened the door, and looked inside.

There was half of a three-day-old mushroom pizza. There were two bananas that had gone completely brown. There were a few slices of bread that were so stale, mold was growing on them. There was an almost empty carton of sour milk. There was half a bottle of flat Dr. Pepper. The smell coming from inside the refrigerator was pretty gross. It smelled like a small animal had died in there.

"I don't think Dad has gone shopping in a while," I said. "I'm going to leave the refrigerator door open awhile to air it out. Why don't we try some of that astronaut food?"

We took out the foil packets of astronaut food we'd bought at the Shlectwasser Air and Space Museum and looked them over. One packet was labeled FREEZE-DRIED PEPPERONI-AND-SAUSAGE PIZZA. I tore open the packet and poured it into a bowl. I carried it over to the kitchen sink and added some water. I mixed it up and tasted it.

"What does it taste like?" Spencer asked.

"Cardboard," I said. "Pepperoni-and-sausage-flavored cardboard."

"Yech," said Spencer. "Let's try another one."

Spencer opened a packet labeled FREEZE-DRIED STRAWBERRY ICE CREAM. He poured it into another bowl, added water and tasted.

"Well?" I said.

"Soap," he said. "It tastes like straw-berry-flavored soap."

"Yum," I said. "My turn."

I took out a packet labeled FREEZE-DRIED S'MORES. Whenever we have campfires, I love making s'mores by melting chocolate, graham crackers and marshmallows together. I wondered how the freeze-dried ones would taste, and then I took a closer look at the packet.

"Oh, rats," I said. "I didn't get s'mores, I got *spores*." I showed Spencer the packet. "Look, Spencer. It says SPORES FROM

MARS. What do you suppose that means?"

In case I haven't mentioned it, Spencer is the smartest kid in our grade. Probably the smartest kid in the Horace Hyde-White School. Probably the smartest kid in the whole entire state of New York. His IQ is around 1,000, I think.

"Spores are kind of like seeds," said Spencer. "They reproduce a lot like seeds. And they're able to survive under lots worse conditions than most seeds."

"What kind of conditions?" I said. "Like a trip from Mars?"

"Spores probably *could* survive a trip from Mars, yeah," said Spencer.

"Hmmm," I said. "Hey, Spencer, do you think these things really came from Mars?"

Spencer shrugged.

"Who knows?" he said. "Maybe they came back on the Mariner probe."

"Mariner never came back from Mars," I said. "Mariner was an unmanned probe designed to stay on Mars."

"You're right," said Spencer. His face turned red.

I had just shown I knew something that the smartest kid in school hadn't known. I felt pretty proud of myself.

"Let's pour this stuff out and see what happens," I said.

I tore open the packet. I poured the spores into another bowl. They looked kind of like seeds, all right. Except weirder. Each spore had two little dark spots on it, like eyes. It was almost as if they were staring at me. That really creeped me out.

"Go ahead," said Spencer. "Add water."

"Uh, OK," I said.

Staring at the spores, I carried the bowl toward the sink. I turned on the faucet and added water. The instant the water hit the spores, I heard a weird hissing sound. Then—and I swear this is the truth— I thought I heard them burp.

I screamed.

The bowl flew out of my hands. I caught it before it hit the floor and broke, but wet spore blobs landed everywhere. Some splattered inside the open refrigerator. Some landed on my computer. Some fell on the floor.

I got a dishrag and tried to mop up what I could.

I looked at what was left in the bowl.

The spores were bubbling now and sticking together to form a pulsing, jelly-like mass. And they were definitely burping.

Spencer came over and looked in the bowl.

"Fascinating," he said. "The spores seem to be growing at a really amazing rate."

It was true. When I poured them in the bowl, they filled only about an eighth of it. And after spilling some, there was even less. But now the bowl was almost half full—the blobby stuff was rising higher and higher.

"Hey, Zack," said Spencer. "Check out the refrigerator."

I looked inside the refrigerator. The pizza was almost gone. So were the brown bananas. So was the moldy bread. The carton of milk was empty.

"Where did all that junk go?" I asked.

The spore globs were spreading on the fridge shelves and climbing up the fridge walls.

"Hey, Spencer, you don't think the spores ate that junky food, do you?"

Spencer looked in the fridge, looked at me, and nodded.

I gulped. "This is really creepy," I said.

"You're not kidding," said Spencer.

Then we heard a weird noise. It came from my computer. I walked over and looked at it. Blobby spore stuff had seeped into my keyboard. There was a message on the screen in the biggest letters I had ever seen. Here's what it said:

"HUMAN BOYS, FEED US. HUMAN BOYS, WE NEED MUCH FOOD NOW."

Chapter 3

"Spencer," I said, "did you do this?"

"Did I do what?"

"Write this on my screen while I wasn't looking?"

"No way," said Spencer.

He looked really scared.

I hooked up the audio on my computer.

"Who is speaking to us on my computer?" I asked.

The computer made a kind of crackling sound. Then I heard a strange, metallic voice:

"HUMAN BOYS, FEED US. HUMAN BOYS, WE NEED MUCH FOOD NOW."

"Who is speaking to us on my computer?" I asked again.

The computer made more crackling sounds. Then we heard the strange, metallic voice again:

"WE ARE SPORES. SPORES FROM MARS."

That *really* creeped me out.

"Mars?" I whispered. "Spencer, how did spores get here from Mars?"

But Spencer was so scared, all he could do was stare at the computer.

"What do you want from us?" I asked.

"FOOD. WE NEED MORE FOOD. WE NEED IT NOW."

"Well, that's all the food we have," I said. "My dad needs to go shopping."

"WHAT IS A DAD? PERHAPS WE CAN EAT A DAD."

"You can't eat my dad," I said. I turned to Spencer. "What should we do here? I think this is getting out of hand." I looked at the fridge. Blobby stuff had dripped down and was spreading all over the kitchen floor.

"YOU MUST GET US MORE FOOD. YOU MUST ALSO DO SOMETHING ELSE FOR US NOW," said the metallic voice.

"What would you like us to do?" Spencer asked.

"GO BACK TO SPACE MUSEUM. BUY MORE SPORES. FREE THEM BY ADDING WATER."

"Why do you want us to free more spores?" Spencer asked.

"MARTIAN SPORES LOVE TO COME TO EARTH, DO TOURIST THINGS."

"What kind of tourist things?" I asked.

"SEE DISNEY WORLD. EAT WHOPPERS AT BURGER KING. GO TO NIKE TOWN AND EAT CROSS-TRAINING

SHOES. MAYBE TAKE OVER THE PLANET EARTH, EAT HUMANS. OOPS, FORGET THAT. MEANT TO SAY MAYBE TAKE PLANTS AND PLANT IN EARTH, MEET HUMANS."

"So spores plan to take over Earth and kill humans?" Spencer asked.

"OH, NO, NO, NOT KILL HUMANS, NEVER KILL HUMANS. JUST, YOU KNOW, GIVE THEM OTHER JOBS."

"Other jobs?" I said. "What kind of other jobs?"

"GOOD JOBS, FUN JOBS."

"Like what?" I asked.

"OH, JOBS LIKE BEING FOOTSTOOLS OR COFFEE TABLES."

"Really?" said Spencer. "Well, for your information, human beings aren't interested in being either footstools or coffee tables for a bunch of stupid Martian spores."

"IF HUMAN BOYS NOT FOLLOW ORDERS, OR IF HUMAN BOYS TELL ANYBODY ABOUT SPORES, THEN BAD THINGS WILL HAPPEN TO HUMAN BOYS."

Spencer and I exchanged nervous looks.

"What kind of bad things?"

"VERY BAD THINGS. DON'T ASK."

"OK," I said. "No problem. We'll go and buy more spores." Then I winked at Spencer so he'd know I didn't mean it. "Well, it's back to the old Shlectwasser Muscum for us. Let's get going."

Chapter 4

When we walked into the Orville and Fanny Shlectwasser Air and Space Museum, the Shlectwassers seemed surprised to see us back so soon.

"Well, hello there, boys," said Mrs. Shlectwasser. "How have you been?"

"Frankly, not all that good," I said. "We need to speak to you about those Martian spores we bought from you."

The Shlectwassers looked nervous.

"What about them?" said Mr. Shlectwasser.

"Well, they were freeze-dried, so we added water," said Spencer. "Then they turned into this disgusting blob that keeps growing and multiplying into more blobs. They started eating everything in sight."

"They ordered us to come back here and buy more freeze-dried spores," I said. "They told us if we didn't, bad things would happen to us. Do you know anything about this?"

Mr. and Mrs. Shlectwasser looked at each other.

"No," said Mr. Shlectwasser.

"No," said Mrs. Shlectwasser.

"You look like you *do* know," said Spencer.

"We just don't want any trouble," said Mr. Shlectwasser.

"We just want to be left alone," said Mrs. Shlectwasser.

"The spores plan to take over planet Earth," I said.

"Well, they wouldn't be the first," said Mr. Shlectwasser.

I sighed. It didn't seem as though the Shlectwassers were going to be much help.

"Isn't there anything you can tell us to help us?" I asked.

"Do what they say," said Mrs. Shlectwasser. "They're not kidding around."

Mr. Shlectwasser motioned to us to move closer. We did.

"You didn't hear this from us." he whispered, "But if you turn a hair dryer on them, it might kill them."

"It's worth a try," I said.

"You didn't hear it from us," said Mrs. Shlechtwasser.

Chapter 5

When Spencer and I got back to Dad's place, the kitchen was a mess. There was globby stuff all over everything. The metallic voice called out from the computer:

"GREETINGS, HUMAN BOYS. DID YOU BUY MORE SPORES?"

"We bought them, we bought them," I said.

"GOOD. NOW ADD WATER."

"In a minute," I said.

Spencer and I went into my bedroom and found a nasty surprise. The spores had eaten my leather dress shoes and my leather sneakers. They had also eaten three leather belts and my baseball mitt. I was madder than anything. I really liked that baseball mitt.

Actually, it was worse than that. There was glop all over my bunk bed and my bureau. It looked like they'd puked up or pooped out some kind of mushy brown stuff and left it all over my floor. Had they done the same in Dad's room? I didn't want to find out.

We were maybe halfway done cleaning up the brown mush on my floor when Dad walked in.

"Hey, Zack, I'm home!" Dad called out. "Are you here?"

Spencer and I walked into the hallway. Dad was carrying two big bags of groceries.

"Oh, hi, Spence," said Dad. "Well, Zack, I finally got us some food."

"Good," I said. "I'm sure the spores will be thrilled."

"The who?"

"The spores."

"Are those the new next-door neighbors?" Dad asked.

"No, these are the spores from Mars," I said. "Wait till you see the kitchen. They're spreading all over our apartment, eating our food, shoes, belts, and my baseball mitt. They want to take over the planet."

Dad laughed.

"Zack is serious, sir," said Spencer. "This apartment *is* crawling with Martian spores. They *have* eaten all those things. And they *are* planning to take over the planet."

Dad put down his grocery bags.

"You want to run that past me again?" he said.

"Dad, listen," I said. "By mistake,

Spencer and I bought some freeze-dried spores from Mars at the Shlectwasser Air and Space Museum, OK? When we added water, they started spreading through our whole apartment. They ate whatever was in the refrigerator. They ate my leather shoes and belts and my baseball mitt. I spilled some on my computer, so they invaded it and can somehow talk to us through it. They told us they plan to take over the planet."

Dad frowned and shook his head.

"I guess this is some kind of put-on you guys are pulling," said Dad. "And I'm sure you find it very funny. But I've had a hard day researching an article I'm writing. I'm kind of tired, and I'm just not in the mood for jokes."

"OK, Dad," I said.

Dad picked up his grocery bags and walked into the kitchen.

"Zack," he called, "why is the refrigerator door open? And what is all this mess? You know I don't mind you boys cooking, but— "

"Dad! It's the spores! They did this!" I yelled."

"I really don't want to hear anymore about spores today," Dad said and headed toward his room. "Just clean up this mess."

"Whatever you say," I answered.

The house intercom buzzed. The doorman said Andrew Clancy was downstairs and wanted to see us. Andrew Clancy is this kid in my class who sometimes has problems with the truth. Spencer and I took the elevator down to the lobby.

"Hey, Andrew," I said. "What's up?"

"I just got your e-mail about the spores," said Andrew.

"What e-mail?" I said. "I didn't send you any e-mail about spores."

"Sure, you did," he said. "You told me to go buy spores. At some place called the Orville and Fanny Shlectwasser Air and Space Museum. What's that about?"

Suddenly I realized what must have happened. I looked at Spencer.

"The spores," I said. "They e-mailed Andrew."

"What?" said Andrew.

"The spores are growing bigger and...smarter," said Spencer. "They're now smart enough to send e-mails."

"Dad has trouble sending e-mails," I said. "You think the spores are now smarter than my dad?"

"What are spores?" Andrew asked.

"Oh, sorry, Andrew," I said. "I forgot you don't know."

"I *do* know," said Andrew. "I just forget sometimes."

"Spores are kind of like seeds," I said.

"They reproduce a lot like seeds. And they're able to survive under lots worse conditions than most seeds."

"Oh, right," said Andrew. "Now I remember. I used to collect spores. In fact, I had spores from almost every state in the union. Where did these come from?"

"Mars," I said.

"Mars, Montana?" said Andrew.

"No, Mars the planet," I said.

"Yeah, I had some of those, too," said Andrew. "But then I traded them for some from Venus."

"Well, just don't buy any more of the ones from Mars," I said. "And let me know if you get any more e-mails about them."

"OK," said Andrew.

Andrew went home. Spencer and I took the elevator back upstairs. When we opened the door, Dad looked more frightened than I have ever seen him.

Zack," he whispered, "something has eaten all my shoes and belts. And your computer has been ordering me around. I thought you and Spencer were kidding about the spores."

"Sir, we would never kid about anything like spores," said Spencer.

"DAD OF HUMAN BOY!" called a metallic voice from the kitchen.

"Uh-oh," said Dad.

"DID WE ORDER YOU TO FEED US MORE OR DID WE NOT!" called the metallic voice.

"I've already fed them a gallon of milk, two quarts of Len and Larry's Cashew Cashew Gesundheit ice cream, four Hungry-Man frozen TV dinners, and a roll of Bounty paper towels," Dad whispered. "I don't know what else I can feed them."

"DAD OF HUMAN BOY!" called the metallic voice.

"Oh, hold your horses!" Dad shouted.

"That's telling them, Dad," I said. "We can't let those stupid spores push us around."

"You're very brave, sir, to yell at spores," said Spencer.

"Well, a man can only take so much," said Dad.

"I think it may be time to get out the you-know-what," said Spencer.

"Oh yes," I said, "let's get the you-know-what."

"What's the you-know-what?" Dad asked.

"Sssshh," said Spencer.

I started moving toward the bathroom.

"Where are you going?" Dad asked.

"To the you-know-where," I whispered.

"What's the you-know-where?" Dad whispered.

"The you-know-where is the place we

keep the you-know-what," I whispered.

Dad frowned. "Oh, right," he said. I don't think he got it, though.

"Zack," said Spencer. "When you go you-know-where to get the you-know-what, be sure to carry it you-know-how, to shield it from the you-know-who's."

"Right," I said. Spencer meant keep the hair dryer hidden, so the spores wouldn't see it.

"DAD OF HUMAN BOY!" called the metallic voice. "ARE YOU GOING TO FEED US NOW, OR ARE WE GOING TO MAKE YOU INTO A SOUVENIR WALL PLAQUE, SUITABLE FOR FRAMING?"

"Keep your shirt on!" Dad yelled.

"BRING US MORE CASHEW CASHEW GESUNDHEIT ICE CREAM!" called the metallic voice.

"You ate all we had!" Dad yelled.

"THEN BRING US MORE BOUNTY

PAPER TOWELS!" called the voice. "THOSE ARE JUST AS TASTY!"

"Fine!" Dad yelled.

I crept down the hall and into the bathroom.

One hair dryer was hanging on the back of the bathroom door. A second one was in a cabinet under the sink. I put both hair dryers under my shirt. I also took a couple of long extension cords. I went back out into the hallway. I have to tell you I was pretty nervous. What would the spores do to me when they discovered I was trying to kill them?

I took the hair dryers out from under my shirt and plugged them into the extension cords. Then I plugged the extension cords into an outlet in the hall.

"DAD OF HUMAN BOY!" called the metallic voice. "WE ARE STILL WAITING FOR OUR BOUNTY PAPER TOWELS!"

"Coming!" Dad called.

I gave one of the hair dryers to Spencer, but he held up his hand.

"I'll stay in the hall," he whispered. "To make sure they don't try and ambush us from the rear."

"Good idea," I whispered. We did need a lookout in the hallway. But I think Spencer was too scared to go into the kitchen with me.

I handed the other hair dryer to Dad and pantomimed firing it at the spores. At first he didn't understand. Then he got it. He smiled at me and gave me the thumbs-up sign.

Together Dad and I walked to the kitchen doorway. We held our hair dryers out in front of us with both hands, just like cops do when they enter a room to capture a bad guy. My heart was beating so hard in my chest I wondered if Dad could hear it.

"You're very brave, son," Dad whispered.

"Thanks, Dad," I said.

"DAD OF HUMAN BOY!" called the metallic voice. "ARE YOUR HEARING ORGANS NONFUNCTIONAL?"

"I'm coming!" Dad yelled. "OK, Zack, let's do it!"

Dad and I jumped into the room like a police SWAT team on TV.

Chapter 6

Right ahead of us on the kitchen floor was a pulsing mass of spores.

I pointed the barrel of my hair dryer at the spores and turned it on "High."

"Take *that*, Martian scum!" I shouted.

The pulsing mass on the floor shuddered. Otherwise it remained about the same.

"What's happening in there?" called Spencer.

"Not too much so far," I said.

Dad threw open the refrigerator door.

There was a mass of spores on the bottom shelf. He pointed his hair dryer at it and fired.

"Take *that,* alien creeps!" he yelled.

Again, the spores shuddered a little, but they looked about the same as they had before I shot them.

I crept up to my computer on the kitchen table. There were spores on my keyboard. I pointed the hair dryer at my keyboard and fired.

"Take *that*, rude and bossy life-forms!" I yelled.

The spores on the keyboard shivered a little, but otherwise they didn't change very much.

"Zack, what's going on?" called Spencer.

"Not a whole lot, if you want to know the truth," I said.

"Should I come in there?" he called.

"Not yet," Dad answered.

Then something happened. All three masses of spores we'd shot with the hair dryer started bubbling.

"Hang on," I called. "They seem to be bubbling now. Spencer, do you think bubbling is a good sign or a bad sign?"

"I think bubbling is a *good* sign," said Spencer.

Suddenly, the three masses of bubbling spores puffed up into bunches of big, transparent bubbles. The bubbles grew to the size of beach balls and you could look right through them. Inside the bubbles were red, spidery things that looked like veins. They looked really gross.

"Uh-oh," said Dad.

The transparent bubbles rose up and floated in the air like jellyfish. Long, stringy tentacles dangled from each of them.

"Uh-oh," I said.

"Bubbling is *probably* a good sign," called Spencer. "Just so long as they don't become something like big, transparent, beach-ball-sized, floating jellyfish with long stringy tentacles dangling from each of them..."

"Uh, Spencer..." I said.

"...because that would mean the heat from the hair dryers hadn't killed the spores, it just energized them enough to morph into their next stage of development."

One of the floating jellyfish was floating in my direction.

"If that happened," Spencer continued, "the one thing you definitely would not want to do..."

I swatted it with my hand. I got a nasty, stinging shock.

"...is touch it," said Spencer. "Because

it might give you a really nasty shock."

I screamed.

"Zack, are you all right?" Dad asked.

"Not really," I said. "It stings. Oww!"

"Let me see," said Dad.

He looked at the hand that got stung. It was starting to swell up.

"We'd better get some ice on that," said Dad.

He went to the freezer compartment and got out some ice trays.

"Did the spores become transparent, beach-ball-sized, floating jellyfish with long tentacles that shocked you?" Spencer called.

"Yes," I said.

"Hmmm," said Spencer. "That's so interesting. My guess is the jellyfish stage would hate any kind of acid. Like vinegar. Do you have any vinegar in there?"

"Dad, do we have any vinegar?" I asked.

My hand really stung from the jellyfish.

"No," said Dad. "But we do have salad dressing with vinegar *in* it."

"That might work," said Spencer.

Dad put ice cubes in a Ziploc bag and put it on my hand. Then he got some bottles of salad dressing out of the cupboard.

Four jellyfish were floating in his direction. Dad stepped forward. He squirted some salad dressing at the dangling tentacles of the closest jellyfish.

The moment the salad dressing hit the tentacles, sparks shot out. The jellyfish shuddered. The air whooshed out of it. Then it shriveled up and dropped to the floor.

"Dad, you did it!" I shouted. "Way to go!"

Dad stepped forward and squirted some more salad dressing. A second jellyfish did the same as the first. It sparked, shuddered, shriveled, and fell to the floor.

"Yay, Dad!" I screamed.

Now the other jellyfish began to float away from Dad. They seemed to know what he was doing.

Even though my stung hand was all swelled up, I took one of the bottles of salad dressing and went after the floating jellyfish. One by one, they shuddered, shriveled, and fell.

Soon, all twelve of them were lying on the floor, in shriveled-up little balls.

"OK, Spencer," I called. "You can come in now!"

Spencer came into the kitchen.

"Those spores were pretty talkative before," I said. "How come they shut up when they became jellyfish?"

"My guess is that Stage Two development of this life-form can't speak," said Spencer.

He stooped over one of the shriveled-up jellyfish and looked at it closely.

"This one is still alive," said Spencer. "Stunned, but still alive." He looked at the others. "Actually they're *all* still alive," he said. "And likely to revive at any moment."

"Oh no! What can we do?" I said.

Chapter 7

Spencer picked up the Yellow Pages phonebook and started looking through it.

"Spencer, what the heck are you doing?"

"We need professional help," he said. "I'm looking under 'Exterminators.' OK, here's an interesting ad. It says 'Bug-Busters. We'll kill anything that bugs you—ants, water bugs, wasps, hornets, termites, roaches, spiders, alien spores. If we're not there in ten minutes, we'll kill it for free.'"

"Boy, you really *can* find anything in the Yellow Pages," said Dad.

Spencer dialed the number.

"Oh, hi," said Spencer into the phone. "We've got alien spores. How soon could you come and exterminate them, and what would you charge? What? Oh, they're from Mars. No, Mars...Well, because it said so on the package. I'm pretty sure they're Stage Two. Right—the transparent beach ball things with the hanging tentacles?"

Spencer looked at us.

"They can be here in ten minutes, and it'll cost $59.99 plus tax," said Spencer.

"Give them our address and tell them to hurry," said Dad.

While we were waiting for BugBusters, I thought we ought to make their job a little easier. We swept all the shriveled-up but living jellyfish on the kitchen floor into a dustpan and dumped them into several large garbage bags. We had just finished when the house intercom buzzed.

Dad turned on the intercom.

"Sir," said the doorman, "there's a SWAT team down here from BugBusters?"

"Send them right up," said Dad.

It wasn't more than nine minutes since Spencer had called. These guys were good.

There was a knock at the door. I went to open it.

In front of me stood three of the most frightening people who have ever come to our front door. They looked like firemen from outer space. They were wearing what looked like black space suits. On the space suits were a red logo with a nasty-looking bug and the letters BB. They had black oxygen tanks on their backs, and big black gloves and boots, and black space helmets

with mirrored visors. They held what looked like black fire extinguishers with the red BB logos.

"We're the BugBusters. Stand back!" said the head BugBuster. His voice sounded miked.

He walked into the living room and blasted a large potted African violet with white foam. The plant immediately shriveled up and died.

"What are you doing?" Dad shouted. "You've just killed my African violet!"

"Aren't you the party who asked us to exterminate the African violets?" said the guy who had just blasted the plant.

"No, we're the party who asked you to exterminate the Martian spores," said Dad. He was really upset.

"OK, OK, just a second here," said the guy. He took a piece of paper out of the pocket of his black space suit. He raised his mirrored visor and squinted at what was written on it.

"All right, my mistake, my mistake," he said. "Couldn't read my own writing. My M's look like A's." He chuckled. "Sorry about that, folks. Now where are those Martian spores?"

"Mostly in the kitchen," I said. "Follow me."

The three BugBusters clomped after me down the hall and into the kitchen. I pointed to the garbage bags.

"They're in there," I said.

The head BugBuster opened the first garbage bag. But before he could blast it with foam, something awful popped out of it. It had a huge mouth full of sharp teeth and large leathery wings. It flew at the head BugBuster.

"It's a Stage Three spore!" yelled one of the other BugBusters.

More of the horrible things started popping out of the garbage bag. All three of the BugBusters opened fire with foam. More of the Stage Three spores hopped out of the garbage bags. The whole kitchen was filled with flapping leathery wings, sharp teeth, and foam.

One flew at me. I picked up a broom and swung it like a baseball bat. I hit the monster with the sweet spot of my bat and blasted a line drive out into the hallway.

Spencer and Dad joined in. For a few minutes, it looked like the battle could go either way, but then the foam started to work. Stage Three spores started dropping like flies. Soon, the whole kitchen was covered in dead Stage Three spores and foam.

The BugBusters went into the hallway, my room, and Dad's room. They blasted all the Stage One spores, and just about every-thing else, including my social studies homework. When they were done, the place was so messed up it would take weeks to put it back together again. But we had won, and the spores were defeated.

"OK, folks," said the head BugBuster. "That'll be $59.99 plus tax and the extra charge for a nighttime service call. All together that comes to...$82.49."

Dad wrote out a check and gave it to the guy.

"That's $82.49," said Dad, handing the head BugBuster the check.

"If you don't mind my saying so," said the head BugBuster, "most of our satisfied customers like to tip us in cash."

"Oh, uh, sure," said Dad. He reached into his pocket and gave each of the BugBusters a ten-dollar bill.

They thanked us and left.

We all flopped down on a sofa in the living room.

"Boy, I'm starved," said Dad. "What do you say we all go out for pizza?"

Spencer and I thought that was a pretty good idea. On the way to the pizza parlor, Spencer, Dad, and I were feeling pretty good about ourselves. We smiled at everyone we passed on the street. Some of them smiled back, but most of them ignored us. Too bad. They might have been a lot friendlier if they'd only known we'd saved them from lives as foot stools, coffee tables or souvenir wall plaques, suitable for framing.

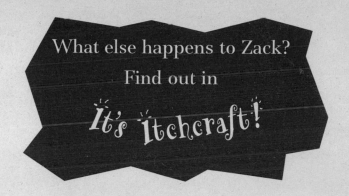

What else happens to Zack?
Find out in
It's Itchcraft!

What else happens to Zack? Find out in *It's Itchcraft!*

My itching got worse. Maybe I had a rash. As soon as I finished talking to Spencer, I went into the bathroom. I took off my shirt and looked in the mirror.

I had a rash all right. Weirdly-shaped red blotches on my chest and back. The blotches looked like letters of the alphabet: B...E...W...and then it went around my side to my back.

I held up my Dad's shaving mirror to read what it said on my back: A...R...E... Oh, no! My rash had spelled out BEWARE!

THE ZACK FILES™

OUT-OF-THIS-WORLD FAN CLUB!

Looking for even more info on all the strange, otherworldly happenings going on in *The Zack Files*? Get the inside scoop by becoming a member of *The Zack Files* Out-Of-This-World Fan Club! Just send in the form below and we'll send you your *Zack Files* Out-Of-This-World Fan Club kit including an official fan club membership card, a really cool *Zack Files* magnet, and a newsletter featuring excerpts from Zack's upcoming paranormal adventures, supernatural news from around the world, puzzles, and more! And as a member you'll continue to receive the newsletter six times a year! The best part is—it's all free!

✂ --

☐ Yes! I want to check out *The Zack Files*
   Out-Of-This-World Fan Club!

name: _____ age: _____

address: _____

city/town: _____ state: ___ zip: _____

Send this form to: Penguin Putnam Books for
                    Young Readers
                    Mass Merchandise Marketing
                    Dept. ZACK
                    345 Hudson Street
                    New York, NY 10014